Dear Parent:
Your child's love of reading starts here!

Every child learns to read in a different way and at his or her own speed. Some go back and forth between reading levels and read favorite books again and again. Others read through each level in order. You can help your young reader improve and become more confident by encouraging his or her own interests and abilities. From books your child reads with you to the first books he or she reads alone, there are I Can Read Books for every stage of reading:

SHARED READING
Basic language, word repetition, and whimsical illustrations, ideal for sharing with your emergent reader

BEGINNING READING
Short sentences, familiar words, and simple concepts for children eager to read on their own

READING WITH HELP
Engaging stories, longer sentences, and language play for developing readers

READING ALONE
Complex plots, challenging vocabulary, and high-interest topics for the independent reader

I Can Read Books have introduced children to the joy of reading since 1957. Featuring award-winning authors and illustrators and a fabulous cast of beloved characters, I Can Read Books set the standard for beginning readers.

A lifetime of discovery begins with the magical words "I Can Read!"

Visit www.icanread.com for information
on enriching your child's reading experience.

To my mom,
who tolerated
all manner of pets
—B.H.

For Parker and Garrett
—G.F.

Clark the Shark Gets a Pet
Copyright © 2020 by HarperCollins Publishers
All rights reserved. Printed in China. No part of this book may be used or reproduced
in any manner whatsoever without written permission except in the case of brief quotations embodied
in critical articles and reviews. For information address HarperCollins Children's Books, a division of
HarperCollins Publishers, 195 Broadway, New York, NY 10007.
www.icanread.com

Library of Congress Control Number: 2020931961
ISBN 978-0-06-291255-8 (trade bdg.)—ISBN 978-0-06-291254-1 (pbk.)

Book design by Chrisila Maida

22 23 24 SCP 10 9 8 7 6 5 4 3 ❖ First Edition

I Can Read!

BEGINNING 1 READING

CLARK THE SHARK
GETS A PET

PET STORE

WRITTEN BY **BRUCE HALE**   ILLUSTRATED BY **GUY FRANCIS**

HARPER
An Imprint of HarperCollinsPublishers

Clark the Shark really wanted a pet.

"Please, Mom, please?" he begged.

"Are you ready?" asked his mother.

"It's a big responsibility."

"I'm already ready!" said Clark.

5

Clark and his mom
looked at all the pets.
Some were too boring.

Some were too weird.

Some were too shocking.

But one pet was just right.

"She likes me!" said Clark.

"Mom, can we take her home?"

"Do you promise to walk her,
feed her, and take care of her?"
asked Clark's mother.

"Yes, yes, and yes!" said Clark.

Clark and his mother

took the dogfish home.

"I'll call you Lulu," said Clark.

Clark gave Lulu some treats,
taught her some tricks,
and played fetch with her.

"Best pet ever!"
cried Clark.

Joey Mackerel came over to play.

"Be good, boys," said Clark's mom.

"We'll be back soon."

"Cool pet!" said Joey.

"Dogfish rock!" said Clark.

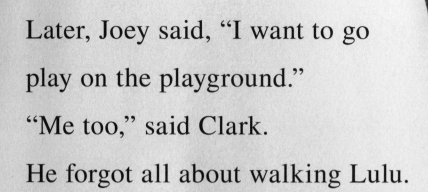

Later, Joey said, "I want to go play on the playground."

"Me too," said Clark.

He forgot all about walking Lulu.

14

Left alone in the house

with too much energy,

Lulu did what lonely pets do.

15

When Mom came home, she was upset.

When Clark came home,

his mother showed him the mess.

"Oh, no!" said Clark. "Bad Lulu!"

"It's not her fault," said his mom.

"That's what happens when you forget to walk your pet."

"I can do better," said Clark.

The next day, Clark walked Lulu
before he went to school.

After school, Clark gave her treats.

But when dinnertime came,
Clark was so busy
watching *SharkBob SquareHead*,
he forgot to feed Lulu.

Later that night,

a loud noise woke Clark.

Lulu had knocked over the trash can

and eaten most of the garbage.

"Mom!" cried Clark.

"Something's wrong with Lulu!"

Clark's mother frowned.

"Did someone forget to feed her?"

she asked.

"Oops," said Clark.

"Um, I can do better."

He tied a string around his fin

to help him remember.

But soon the string fell off.

The next evening, Clark was so busy

with his school project,

he forgot to play with Lulu.

That night, Lulu kept everyone awake
with her howling, her whining,
and her rough-and-tumble racket.

"She needs to play," said Clark's mom.

"You're not being fair to your pet."

"I love my sweet Lulu," said Clark,

"but I can't remember what to do."

"Hey, that rhymes," said his mother.

Clark smiled. He liked rhymes.

Hmm . . .

Clark thought long and hard.

There was so much to remember.

Could one rhyme cover it all?

There was only one way to find out!

Clark said:

"If you want to keep a pet,

these are things you can't forget:

walk and feed and love and play,

then your pet will want to stay."

That's exactly what he did.

And soon, Lulu and Clark became
the very best of friends.

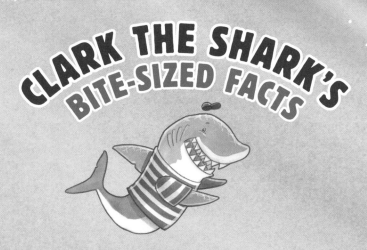

CLARK THE SHARK'S BITE-SIZED FACTS

1 Some fish have animal names, but they don't look like the animals they're named after! Besides dogfish, there are also catfish, seahorses, and even lionfish!

2 Dogfish aren't just fish . . . they're a type of shark!

3 Sometimes you can teach your pet fish tricks! With the right training, a fish can learn to go through hoops and weave through poles, and even play fetch.